A Purnell book
ISBN 0 361 03483 0
First published 1976. Reprinted 1987
Copyright © 1976 Express Newspapers plc
Printed by Purnell Book Production Ltd
Paulton, Bristol. A member of BPCC plc
Macdonald & Co (Publishers) Ltd
Greater London House, Hampstead Road
London NW1 7QX. A BPCC plc company

RUPERT
and the Carved Stick

Illustrated by Bestall
Based on his original story

Purnell

CHAPTER 1

For several weeks Rupert's Daddy had been bringing home brightly coloured booklets in his briefcase. Rupert had seen them when his Daddy opened his case, and once he had asked what they were all about.

"Oh, we're trying to decide where to go on our holidays," said Mrs Bear. Then she sighed. "But all the holidays are so expensive that I don't think we'll be able to afford it."

Rupert felt very sorry then, because he liked going on holiday.

"Never mind, though," he said to his Mummy. "There are lots of nice places around Nutwood that I've never been to, I'm sure we'll find plenty to do."

"What a kind little bear you are!" said his Mummy. "And do you know, you've given me an idea!"

She wouldn't tell Rupert what the idea was, but he was soon to find out.

One Saturday morning not long after, Rupert was helping his Mummy in the kitchen when a strange rattling noise began outside. It grew louder and louder, as if some funny monster was coming down the road. Then, suddenly, it gave a loud 'pop' and a snort, and everything went quiet.

"I'll go and see what it is!" shouted Rupert, and he raced out into the garden.

There, by the front gate, stood a very old car. Rupert had never seen one quite as old before! While he was looking at it, a man got out of the driver's seat and came across to him.

"Is this Mr Bear's house?" he asked.

"Yes, it is," said Rupert. "I'll go and call him."

Mr Bear hurried out to see the man, with Rupert close behind him.

"Dear me, is this it?" he said.

"It was the only one we had for the price you wanted to pay," said the man. "But don't worry—it goes all right if you make sure it's not overloaded and that the oil and water are topped up."

"Thank you very much," said Mr Bear, and the man nodded to Rupert and went away.

"Is this car ours?" cried Rupert. "Have you bought it, Daddy?"

"No, but I've hired it for a couple of weeks

so that we can all go out on day trips," said Mr Bear. "Look, here comes your mother now, so we'll have a look inside, shall we?"

Mr and Mrs Bear and Rupert climbed inside and sat on the seats. As they did so the little car went 'boing!'

"Listen, it's talking to us!" said Rupert. "Oh, Daddy, I *do* like this car! What a good idea it was of yours to hire it!"

"Well, it was your idea really," said Mrs Bear. "You said that there were lots of nearby places you hadn't seen."

"Tomorrow we'll pack a picnic basket and go out for the day," said Mr Bear as he helped Rupert's Mummy out of the car. "I don't know where we'll go, but it will be fun, won't it?"

"Oh yes!" said Rupert. "I can hardly wait!"

"I don't think we should go if it's raining," said Mrs Bear. "Picnics aren't much fun in the rain."

"Oh dear!" said Rupert. "I hadn't thought of that!"

But when morning came, Rupert found that he needn't have worried. The sun was shining brightly and when he came down into the kitchen he found that his Mummy had already been very busy. She had made lots of sandwiches and little cakes, and was putting them into the picnic hamper alongside a flask of tea and some fruit.

"What a lot of food!" cried Rupert.

"Yes, I think I've made more sandwiches than ever your father can eat," laughed Mrs Bear. "I don't know what we'll do with them all!"

"Oh, can I take one of my pals with me, then?" said Rupert. "Please say yes!"

Mrs Bear looked doubtful.

"Well, the car is very old . . . but I expect it

would hold another person. Now sit down and have your breakfast, and then you can go and see who would like to come with us."

After breakfast Rupert ran outside to see which of his friends was around. But there was nobody in sight!

"Oh dear!" sighed the little bear. "I hope some-  one comes along soon, because we'll waste all morning if I'm not quick!"

Just then his friend, Edward Trunk, appeared on the common, pushing his baby brother in a pushchair.

"Hello, Edward! How would you like to go on a picnic with me?" cried Rupert.

"Oh, I'd love to!" said Edward. "Thank you ever so much for asking me, Rupert!"

"It's a surprise sort of picnic, because we don't know where we'll be having it," said Rupert. "You see, my Daddy's hired a car, and we're just going to drive until we find a nice spot. I say, shouldn't you take your baby brother home first?"

"Oh, I'll have to bring him with me!" said Edward, anxiously. "I hope that's all right. You see, my parents have left me in charge of him for the day. He's no trouble, are you, Pompey? And he doesn't eat much— well, not as much as I do."

"It's not that," said Rupert. "It's just that . . . well, the car is very old and it may not take another person as well as you. We'll have to ask Mummy."

Mrs Bear looked very worried when she found that two little elephants wanted to join in the picnic party.

"Oh, do let's try it!" cried Rupert. "Let's

all get into the car and see what it says about it. You know it talks to us!"

So everyone piled into the little car. 'Boing!' it said, as Mr Bear got in. 'Boing!' it said, as Mrs Bear got in. 'Boing!' it said as Rupert got in. And 'Boing *boing*!' it said, as Edward and Pompey got in too.

For a moment it seemed to be making up its mind, but then, suddenly, its puttering engine started to shout.

'Vroom, vroooommmm!' said the little car, and everyone breathed a sigh of relief.

"I think it likes us!" said Edward, happily. "Oh look, Algy and Bill are running across the common to see us!"

Rupert looked out and waved to his friends.

"Hello, you two!" he called.

"Hello, Rupert! Hello, Edward!" said Algy. "Are you going on a picnic? I wish we could come too!"

"Sorry, full up!" laughed Mr Bear. "You should have got here earlier! Well, we must be going, before this little car changes its mind!"

"Have a nice time!" shouted Bill, as the car rattled away.

"We will!" called Rupert. And then he and Edward forgot about everything except looking out of the window to see where they were going.

"I think we'd better keep to the side roads, just in case the car gets tired," said Mr Bear. So they chugged along through leafy, winding lanes, for most of the morning.

"I'm getting hungry!" said Rupert, at last.

"Me too!" agreed Edward.

"Din-dins!" cried Pompey.

"Not much further

now," said Mr Bear. "We're nearly there."

"I can see the sea!" Rupert cried. "Look, everybody—by that ruined castle, through the trees!"

"I thought we would reach it soon," smiled Mr Bear. "I didn't tell you where I was heading for in case the car broke down. But it didn't! In fact it's rather a good little car. I'm very pleased with it."

"There's a nice patch of green grass just there, dear, for picnicking on," suggested Mrs Bear. "Are we allowed to stop here?"

"I don't see why not," said Mr Bear, and he parked the car carefully off the road.

CHAPTER 2

Everyone climbed out and, while Mr Bear gave the car a long drink of water, Rupert and Edward helped Mrs Bear to spread a cloth on the ground and to lay out the picnic. Pompey sat and watched them, clapping his hands with delight.

"I must say, he's a very good baby," said Mrs Bear. 'Hasn't your mother brought him up well, Edward!"

"I'll tell her you said so, Mrs Bear," said Edward. "I'll sit next to him and help him eat his sandwiches."

"Come along, Daddy!" called Rupert. And soon everyone was tucking into the delicious spread.

There was silence for a while, for everyone was too busy eating to talk, but after the meal, when Edward had mopped up Pompey and Mr Bear had settled down comfortably to an after-dinner snooze, Rupert looked around him and realised that they were very near to the ruined castle.

"I wonder if we could walk there?" he said, excitedly.

"I couldn't walk anywhere after all that food!" said Mr Bear, without opening his eyes.

"Oh, but it would be *fun*," sighed Edward. 'I've never been inside a ruined castle in my life! You never know what you're going to find—perhaps there's even some buried treasure!"

Mrs Bear laughed. "I can see you're very excited by the thought of it, Edward," she said. "And, as you've been such good boys this morning, I don't see why you and Rupert shouldn't go exploring if you want to."

19

"Oh, Mrs Bear, do you mean it?" cried Edward.

"Yes, if you promise to be careful, and not try climbing up the walls," replied Mrs Bear. "Pompey can stay here with us—he'll be quite all right. Wake up, Daddy, and pass the baby over to me."

"We won't be long—and we will be careful!" said Rupert, as they scampered off.

It didn't take long to reach the castle.

"What a terrible state it's in!" said Edward.

"I think I know why," said Rupert. "This must be Old Lady Witterham's castle. Her son went to live abroad and some years later she joined him. That's why everything is in ruins. Algy was telling me about it, because his mother read something in the newspaper about the son, Sir Robert Witterham, coming back to this country to sort out his mother's affairs."

"Oh, I remember now," said Edward. "It was in the Nutwood Gazette. Sir Robert said that he was afraid that the castle and grounds would have to be sold. Fancy having to sell a place like this! First rate for hide and seek games! Oh, Rupert, just look at that dear little island over there!"

Rupert shaded his eyes from the sun with is hand and gazed out to sea.

"Yes, it's a perfect little hide-out," he agreed. "Wouldn't it be lovely to explore *that*!"

"How would we get out to it?" said Edward.

."We can't," said Rupert. "I was only joking! Anyway, there isn't time."

"What a shame," said Edward, sadly.

"Cheer up!" said Rupert. "We came her to explore the old ruined castle, remember? And now you want to explore something else!"

Edward laughed and moved away from the edge of the cliff.

"Phew, I'm glad you did that!" said Rupert. "I didn't like to say anything in case I frightened you, but you were awfully near the edge just then."

CHAPTER 3

The two friends hurried off to explore among the broken walls and mossy hollows of the old castle. Rupert wandered away for a few minutes, but suddenly heard Edward's voice calling him.

"Rupert! Come back here a minute, I've found something!" Edward was shouting.

"What have you found?" asked Rupert, calling back.

"Well, it's a . . . it looks like a . . . well, if you come back, you'll see!" called Edward.

Rupert returned to his friend at once.

"Why, it's only a walking stick!" he exclaimed, when he realised what Edward was looking at. "I expect some hiker left it by mistake."

"It's not just any old walking stick!" retorted Edward. "Take a closer look at it!"

Rupert walked forward and picked up the stick.

"Why, it's carved from end to end!" he said. "I see what you mean! It *is* a fine stick and no hiker would be careless enough to leave it lying around like this. I say, are those words carved into the wood?"

"Yes, and even the handle has something carved on it," said Edward. "Looks like a set of numbers—yes, it is! 7326514 . . . now what can *that* mean?"

"Don't ask me!" said Rupert. "It isn't a year and it can't be somebody's age."

Deep in thought, the two friends walked on.

"Perhaps it's a telephone number?" suggested Edward. "Though who would want to carve a telephone number on a walking stick? Suppose the people at the exchange decided to change the number? It would be awfully difficult to change the numbers on the stick."

So busy were they with their thoughts that neither of the pals realised that they were being watched by a gentleman just ahead of them.

"Hey—do you know you're trespassing?" he called. The two pals looked up, startled.

"I'm terribly sorry," said Rupert, "but we aren't doing any harm, really. We're on a picnic and the castle looked so interesing that we just had to explore."

The man chuckled.

25

"Yes, I can remember I thought it did when I was a boy. Of course, it wasn't ruined then, at least not all of it. I can't believe that I shall really have to sell it at last."

The friends gasped.

"Do you own it, then?" said Rupert. "You must be . . ."

"Sir Robert Witterham is my name," said the gentleman. "Yes, it's true, I'm afraid. I own it—but I can't afford to keep it up. It costs so much to start repairs. I even went abroad to try to make my fortune, so that I could return one day a wealthy man and restore the castle to its former glory. But I didn't make my fortune and now the castle is more derelict than ever. If only I could find the family silver that an ancestor is supposed to have hidden! One piece of that would be enough to raise the money I need to save the castle."

"Can we help you look for it? We've got a few minutes to spare," said Edward.

"Thank you for offering, but it has been

hidden for centuries, and I don't think we'd find it," said Sir Robert. "I say, where did you find that stick? I've been looking for it for days!"

Edward explained that they had found it only a few yards away.

"I'm very grateful to you for finding it for me," said Sir Robert. "It's been in the family for donkey's years and I would have hated to lose it."

"What do all the numbers mean on it?" asked Rupert. "Is it a telephone number?"

"I shouldn't think so," said Sir Robert. "This stick belonged to my grandfather and he lived before the days of telephones. I

believe it is even older than that. I've no idea what the words mean, either."

While the pals listened he read the words out to them.

"Highest - rock - shall - give - to - oak - the - point - line - and - the - silver - oak."

"But that doesn't make sense!" said Edward.

"I know," agreed Sir Robert. "I've puzzled over those words quite a bit. My grandfather never knew what they meant, either."

"I'm afraid we have to go now," said Rupert. "My Mummy and Daddy will be wondering where we are."

"Nice to have met you," said Sir Robert. "I—oh!"

As he spoke, the cliff edge crumbled beneath

his feet and, lurching forward, he only just managed to save himself.

"That was a nasty scare!" he said turning to look down at the rocks below.

"Are you all right?" asked Rupert. "Edward nearly did the same thing a little while ago. I say—where's your stick?"

"I must have dropped it over the edge when I jumped clear!" said Sir Robert, unhappily. "Oh, dear! I would hate to lose it!"

"Don't worry, we'll go and look for it!" offered Rupert.

"That's very kind of you," said Sir Robert.

It took quite a while for the friends to scramble down the rocky path, but at last they reached the rocks below.

"There's the stick— between those two large rocks over there!" shouted Edward suddenly. "Look, it's standing up straight in the air."

But they found it was firmly wedged in a small crack in the rocks.

"Oh!" exclaimed Rupert, as he tugged at the stick. "The end moved! I do believe it unscrews!'' he cried excitedly.

Sure enough, the end of the stick unscrewed from the rest of it. When they looked closely at it they found that it had the word OAK carved on it.

"Let me have one last try at freeing it," said Edward. So he took a firm grip and pulled . . . and pulled . . . and pulled.

Out came the stick from the rocks!

"Well done, Edward! You *are* strong!" said Rupert.

They took the stick back to Sir Robert. He was very surprised to find that the end unscrewed, and they left him studying it intently.

Rupert and Edward ran back to Mr and Mrs Bear.

"We met the owner of the castle, Mummy," said Rupert, "and—"

Just then Sir Robert himself appeared, waving his stick and shouting.

"Please wait a minute!" he gasped. "You have been so useful to me

that I should like to meet you again. Where do you live?"

"I'm glad these youngsters haven't been making nuisances of themselves," said Mr Bear. "We live in Nutwood."

Sir Robert waved as they drove away, and Rupert and Edward told Mr and Mrs Bear all about the carved stick.

Next morning, while Rupert was eating his breakfast, there was a knock on the door. Mrs Bear went to answer it.

"Why, it's Sir Robert!" she exclaimed.

"Good morning, Mrs Bear," smiled Sir Robert. "Would you mind if Rupert spent the day with me? I've got something very interesting to show him and I've brought my car to take him."

"Gosh, am I going for a ride in that?" said Rupert. "Is Edward coming too? Have you found the missing silver?"

"What a lot of questions!" laughed Sir Robert, as he opened the car door for Rupert. Edward was already sitting inside!

CHAPTER 4

When they arrived at his big house, Sir Robert disappeared and then returned with the stick and came across to the table where they sat.

"I think I've discovered a message from the writing on the stick!" he said. He was just as excited as Rupert and Edward. "Look . . . here are the numbers on the handle."

"7326514," Edward read, aloud. "There are seven figures in all."

"Yes—and there are seven sections on the stick!" said Sir Robert.

"I begin to see what you mean!" said Rupert. "What happens if you put the sections of the stick into the order of the

33

numbers on the handle?"

"You're a clever little bear!" laughed Sir Robert. "Here's the stick—you try it!"

Nobody spoke as Rupert carefully un-screwed the seven sections of the stick and laid them out on the table. Slowly he juggled them around until they were all in their new positions. Then he gave a loud shout and danced around the room.

"That's it! We've done it! Hurray!" he shouted.

"You might stop prancing around and tell me what's going on!" said Edward, indignantly. "What does the stick say now? Does it make sense?"

"It says: *Oak to oak shall give the silver line and highest rock the point*," said Rupert. "I don't know what it means but it sounds

34

more sensible than it did before."

"It certainly does!" agreed Sir Robert. "And what is more, I think I've worked out what it means."

Rupert and Edward were very excited and

followed Sir Robert out of the house. He led them to the ruins of the old castle.

"I can't see any oak trees," said Rupert.

"No—but you're standing on the stump of one!" said Sir Robert.

"And there is another stump over there," he added pointing to a spot not far away. "Stay where you are, Rupert, and you,

Edward, go and stand on the other one, please."

As Edward ran towards the other stump, Rupert said:

"I suppose, when the stick was carved, these two oaks were still growing?"

"That's right!" said Sir Robert. "Good, there's Edward on the other stump. Now—the line from you to him must be the silver line . . . and we must look for a high point. But there seems to be only flat ground between you and Edward."

"Just a minute!" shouted Rupert. "If I look *past* Edward, I can see your island out to sea!"

Sir Robert stood behind Rupert and peered past Edward at the island.

"I do believe you're right, little bear!" he exclaimed.

Edward was thrilled when he heard that the *highest point* in the clue seemed to refer to the island.

"I knew there was something exciting about that island!" he said. "But I never dreamed it would be a *treasure* island!"

"Can we get out to it, Sir Robert?" asked Rupert, eagerly.

"Yes, I have a rowing boat moored beneath the cliff," said Sir Robert.

"What an adventure this has turned out to be!" said Rupert as Sir Robert steered the boat into a tiny cove between the rocks on the island.

The boat bumped to a halt and Rupert and Edward scrambled out on to the rocks.

"I don't think I can manage on these rocks," said Sir Robert.

CHAPTER 5

Rupert and Edward left Sir Robert in the boat and began to climb up the rocks.

"Don't go so fast, Rupert!" gasped Edward. "I'm fatter than you and I can't keep up!"

"Don't worry—I'll wait for you at the top!" laughed Rupert. And at last, panting for breath, Edward joined him on a large, flat rock at the very top of the island.

"The carved stick said that the highest rock gives the point where the silver is hidden, and we are standing on the highest rock," said Rupert.

Edward glanced down at the rock beneath his feet.

"Hey, Rupert, I believe something is carved on the stone of this rock!" he said, suddenly.

"Get off a minute and let's have a look."

Sure enough, there was a thin line cut into the stone.

"Look, Edward—it's the shape of the carved stick!" said Rupert. "We must be on the right track!"

"Perhaps . . . perhaps it's pointing to something," said Edward, slowly. "Why, there's a smaller boulder there, jammed against this big rock. Do you think we could move it?"

"*You* might be able to, Edward!" laughed Rupert. "You're bigger than me—and stronger. Shall we try it!"

Edward knelt down beside the boulder and tried to push it with his shoulder.

"Gosh, it feels as if it hasn't been moved for years!" he said, panting for breath. "Wait a minute. I'll push with my feet, and you help."

Suddenly the boulder wobbled and fell away from the big, flat rock.

"Well done, Edward!" shouted Rupert.

"Hey, there's a hole where the boulder was!" said Edward. Both of them dived towards it.

"Ouch!" they both said, together, as they hit their heads against each other.

"Tell you what," said Rupert, "I'll explore while you stay here . . . Edward?"

But Edward had already disappeared into the hole!

"Where are you, Edward?" shouted Rupert down the hole.

"I fell in!" called Edward. His voice sounded a very long way away.

"Goodness!" thought Rupert to himself. "That hole must be very deep!" Aloud, he shouted:

"Don't worry, Edward! I'm going to get help!"

Quickly, Rupert scrambled over the rocks until he reached the boat. Sir Robert was sitting in the stern, but when he saw Rupert scurrying towards him he stood up, rocking the boat so that he nearly fell over.

"Where's your friend, little bear? Are you all right? What's happening?"

Rupert explained what had happened.

"Goodness me, I hope Edward hasn't hurt himself!" said Sir Robert. "Here, there's a rope in this boat. Take it back to the hole, tie one end firmly round something, and see if he can climb up it."

Back at the high rock, Rupert wasted no time in fixing the rope to the boulder.

"Hey, Edward, are you there?" he called, down the hole.

"Course I am!" shouted Edward.

"There's a rope coming down!" called Rupert. Down went the rope—and before long, up came Edward!

"Phew, I'm out of breath—I'm not a monkey, I'm an elephant, and elephants don't often climb ropes!" he gasped, as Rupert helped him roll out of the hole. "But . . . I say, Rupert, I think I've found the missing silver! There's an old chest down there nearly as big as me!"

When Sir Robert heard the news he rowed quickly back to the mainland.

"This *is* exciting!" he said. "You've done very well indeed! Now I'm taking you back to my house, and I'll get my gardener to see about the chest!"

When they arrived, the two pals were very hungry, and the housekeeper bustled about preparing them a lovely tea.

They were tucking into crumpets dripping with butter and supping large mugs of tea when into the kitchen came Sir Robert.

"You were right—the silver *was* in that chest at the bottom of the hole!" he said. "My gardener is just bringing it into the hall."

Rupert and Edward ran into the hall just as the gardener was opening the lid of the trunk.

Everyone gasped as the silver was taken out and spread on the floor. There were goblets and vases, plates and jugs of all shapes and sizes.

"This will fetch enough money to enable me to restore the castle to good condition!" exclaimed Sir Robert. "Thank you, Rupert and Edward! Thank you for finding the silver and saving the castle!"

It was a very tired Rupert who flopped into his own bed that night.

"Well, it was fun, but I expect that's the last I shall hear of Sir Robert and his silver," he thought to himself.

But he was wrong. Several days passed, and then one morning he looked out across the common to see Edward hurrying towards his house.

He opened the bedroom window and called out to him.

"Hello, Edward! You're up early this morning!"

"Hello, Rupert! Have you got yours?" shouted Edward, waving a piece of paper.

"My what?" asked Rupert, puzzled. But Edward was too out of breath to say any more. Rupert ran downstairs and on the mat was a white envelope addressed to him. He picked it up and opened the door for Edward.

"That's it!" said Edward, coming up the path. "Open it up, Rupert!"

It was a letter from Sir Robert, and a card requesting the pleasure of Mr and Mrs Bear and Rupert at Nutchester Museum that very day. The letter read:

'Dear Rupert,

'I hope to see you at the Museum today. All news then.

Yours,
Sir Robert.'

"Just what mine said!" cried Edward. "Except that it began 'Dear Edward'."

At two o'clock they all set out for the museum. And when they got there they were amazed to find that a crowd of people were waiting to make a tremendous fuss of them. People were taking their photographs, and television cameras were whirring. Sir Robert was there, wearing his very best clothes, and all the gleaming silver was displayed in a large showcase. It looked magnificent.

"My family treasure restored, and it's all thanks to you!" said Sir Robert.